First published in the United States by Dial Books for Young Readers
2 Park Avenue · New York, New York 10016

Published in the Netherlands 1987 by Lemniscaat Publishers
Published simultaneously in Canada by Fitzhenry & Whiteside Limited, Toronto
Copyright © 1987 by Lemniscaat b. v. Rotterdam
All rights reserved
Printed and bound in Belgium
First Edition
COBE
2 4 6 8 10 9 7 5 3 1

Library of Congress Cataloging-in-Publication Data

Schubert, Dieter, 1947-   Where's my monkey?
Summary: Through a wordless chain of events, a boy's toy monkey
is lost in a rainstorm and retrieved only after it passes
through many hands.
[1. Toys—Fiction. 2. Lost and found possessions—Fiction.
3. Stories without words.] I. Title.
PZ7.S3829Wh 1987   [E]   86-16578
ISBN 0-8037-0069-5

Where's My Monkey?

✤ *Dieter Schubert* ✤

Dial Books for Young Readers · *New York*

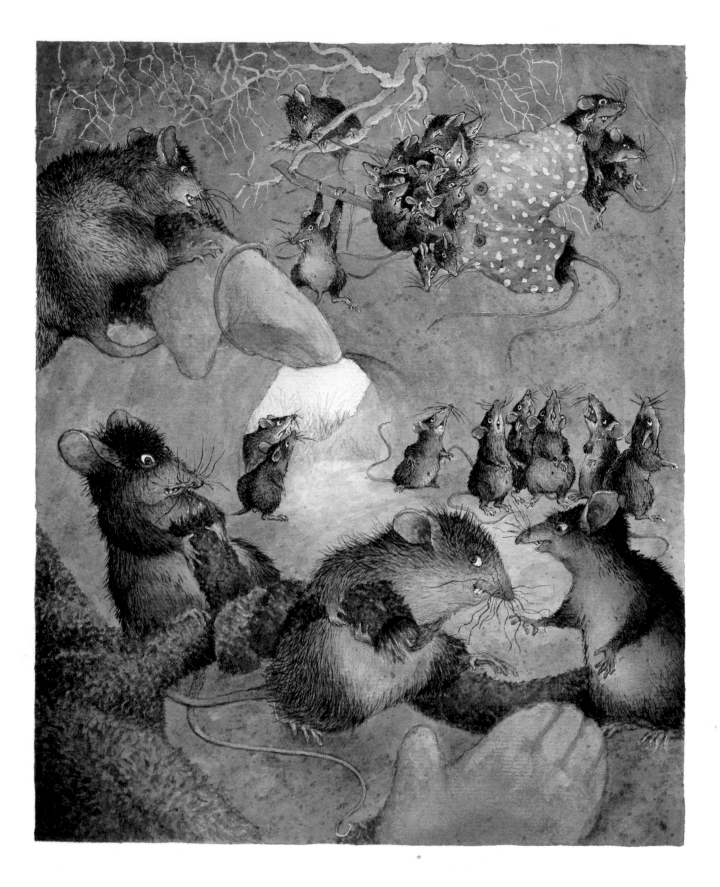

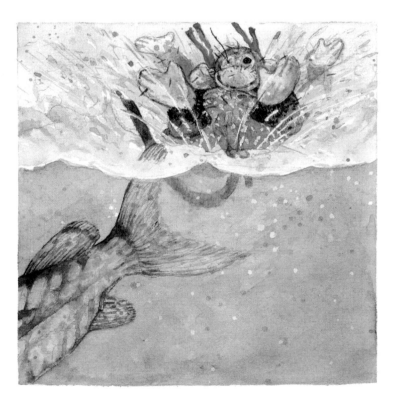

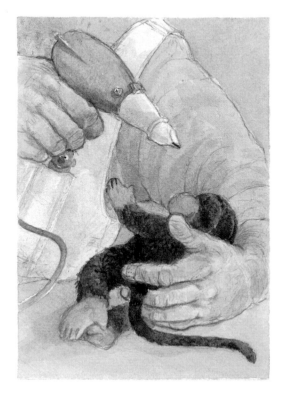

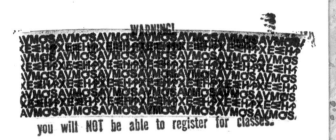